Zaagi
and
Biboonkeonini

Written by Allie Tibbetts

Illustrations by Sam Zimmerman

Zaagi looked outside. Yesterday the snow had melted just enough to catch a glimpse of the grass, but today a mountain of snow stood again. She shook her fist at the snow.

"It's almost my birthday, and there is snow everywhere!" she wailed. "I want to play in the dirt!"

"Ninga (my Mom) said that Biboonkeonini (Wintermaker) is still in the sky," her cousin, Cyrus, told her. "So there is still snow, but who cares, Zaagi? Maanoo (don't care, let it be)." He pulled on his boots and went stomping through the snow, leaving Zaagi glaring after him.

He came back in later, red-cheeked, to find Zaagi sulking.

"Howah," he said. "Get over it, will you?"

"Gaawiin! (No!)" she snapped. "I have things I want to do." She wanted to jump in a puddle or find a worm at least. Cyrus knew Zaagi was sad. He sat next to her.

"Hey, Zaagi," he said, "Grandpa told me a story once."

Zaagi left her thoughts to look at her cousin. "Yeah?" she said curiously.

"Yeah," said Cyrus. "He said that children can take their bows and arrows and shoot at Biboonkeonini up there in the sky and it'll make him go away faster. So maybe if you go see him tonight, you can shoot him right out of the sky! Then you can play in the dirt."

Zaagi thought for a moment. Brightened, she hugged her cousin.

"That's what I'll do! If Biboonkeonini won't leave on his own, I'll make him leave!" she vowed.

Late that night, Zaagi took her bow and all the arrows she could find. She hoped it would be enough to drive Biboonkeonini away. She braced herself against the cold winter air of the night as she went outside. Zaagi faced the west and began shooting, one after another, as fast as she could.

In the flurry of arrows, there was barely an icy swish from the sky and suddenly Biboonkeonini was in front of her, a cold, looming figure. He stood tall and unmoving but for the swirls of frosty snow encircling him, still in movement from the journey from the stars above. Zaagi's breath caught at the sight of him.

He shifted and slivers of ice fell from him in a shimmer. He looked at her, and she looked back at him. Now she could tell him what she really thought, how she really felt about this winter he refused to end. But when she looked at Biboonkeonini, she paused and peered at him curiously. His eyes looked heart-achingly sad. She opened her mouth to speak, less angry now but still firm.

"Biboon has lasted long enough," she said. "The goon (snow) has been with us for too long. I want to play outside in the sun. I want to see the grass. I want the ice to melt to go in the zaaga'igan (lake). I want to hear maang (loon), see a flower, a bee, see something besides this white blanket you have set on us all these months." She glared at him then, her anger returning.

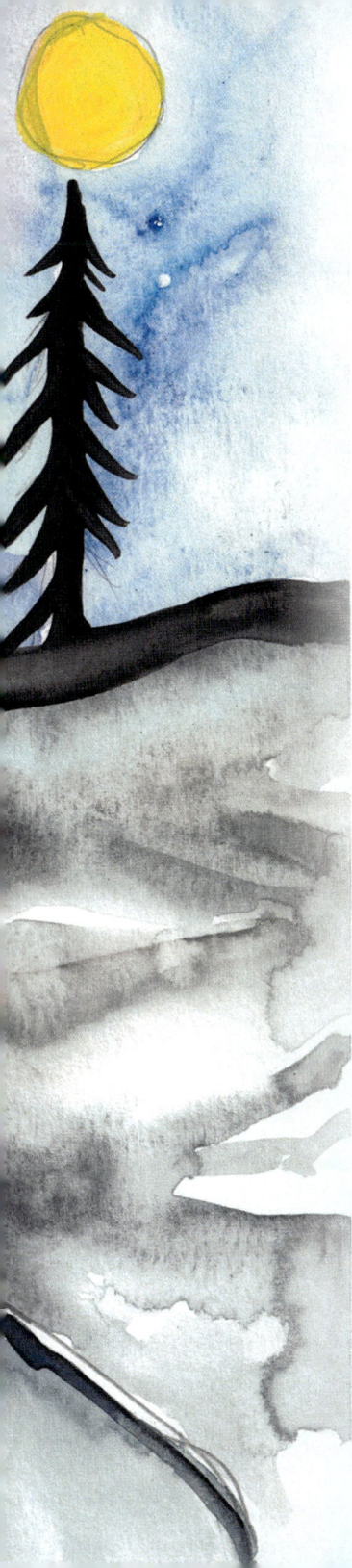

Biboonkeonini raised his eyebrows and spoke, icy shards falling from the corners of his lips.

"Without me, you wouldn't get to tell your aadizookaanag (sacred stories) that you need the snow on the ground to tell. You wouldn't get to enjoy the zaaga'iganan (the lakes). The long winter keeps the waters clean and fresh. You wouldn't get your rest in the winter," he said.

"I don't like to rest," Zaagi argued, but her anger was fading. Biboonkeonini had a point about the stories and the water, she thought before looking back at him. His eyes were cast far away and still so sad.

"Why are you sad?" Zaagi asked. "You live among the stars and see things we never get to see!" she exclaimed, waving to the cosmos. She'd love to be in the stars sometime, in the silence of space to see all there is to see.

"You, too, see things I never get to see," Biboonkeonini said. "I don't get to see the plants grow, hear maang, see a flower, a bee, not anything besides this white blanket of snow."

"You don't get to see a flower?" Zaagi asked in disbelief. He shook his head and snowflakes flew.

"I'm long gone by the time they come," he said. Zaagi's heart felt sad for him. She loved the waabigwaniin, the flowers. And to think Biboonkeonini never saw anything but the snow! He continued, "I make the snow and let the people and the earth rest in it and the children play. At the beginning of winter, people are so happy to see the snow, but then some forget how beautiful it is by the end. And worse still, I have others shooting at me."

"Maybe I won't shoot my arrows at you anymore," Zaagi said softly.

Biboonkeonini laughed and said, "Zaagi, there is something to dislike and something to like in any season. Winter may be long but it is forever for me. It is not forever for you."

They offered each other a smile and with another swish as swift as the first, he was gone. She looked to the west where he was traveling further down in the sky, about to depart for the spring, and saw him there, twinkling.

The next morning, Zaagi awoke to snowflakes falling light and slow in the sky. She sighed, but she put on her winter clothes and headed outside. She caught some snowflakes in her mouth and then went walking in the woods. She could see so far without the leaves covering the trees and brush. Soon I won't be able to see that far, she thought. She packed some snowballs and flung them through the woods. She crunched her feet through the crust on the snow and noticed how that was the only noise she could hear. Maybe winter is as quiet as the stars, she thought. And when the day fell and night emerged, she smiled up at Biboonkeonini. He twinkled back at her.

When spring came, Zaagi saw the leaves and flowers budding. Zaagibagaa. One sunny day, she made a little plate with some manoomin (wild rice) and zhiiwaagamizigan (maple syrup). She found a flower. Zaagi took her asemaa (tobacco) and put it down as she picked the flower and placed it on the plate. Setting it at a tree, she spoke.

"Here, Biboonkeonini, here is some of spring for you to enjoy," she announced. A cool wind rushed over her. "Don't even!" she laughed. "You'll be back soon enough."

Zaagi faced the sky and let the sun shine on her. Spring was here.

Ojibwemowin Glossary

Zaagi'—love, treasure him or her

Biboonkeonini—Wintermaker

Ninga—My Mom

Maanoo—don't; don't care; let it be; never mind

Biboon—it is winter

Goon—snow

Zaaga'igan(an)—lake(s)

Maang—loon

Aadizookaanag—sacred stories

Waabigwaniin—flowers

Zaagibagaa—it buds; the leaves come out

Manoomin—wild rice

Zhiiwaagamizigan—maple syrup

Asemaa—tobacco

Biboonkeonini

Biboonkeonini, or Wintermaker, is the manidoo (spirit) of biboon (winter). Wintermaker's significance is conveyed through his name; he brings the winter. Biboonkeonini is an Ojibwe winter constellation, visible overhead in the southern night sky during the winter months where the commonly known Greek constellation of Orion is located. Biboonkeonini's outstretched arms reach far beyond into other stars across the sky.

For my daughter—
my love for you stretches the sky
like Wintermaker

Zaagi and Biboonkeonini

©2023 by Allie Tibbetts, Illustrations by Sam Zimmerman

ISBN 978-1-7369493-4-4

Book cover and interior design by Paul Nylander | Illustrada

Black Bears and Blueberries Publishing
www.blackbearsandblueberries.com

A Native owned non-profit publishing company, with a focus on creating and developing Native children's books for all young people written by Native writers and illustrated by Native artists.

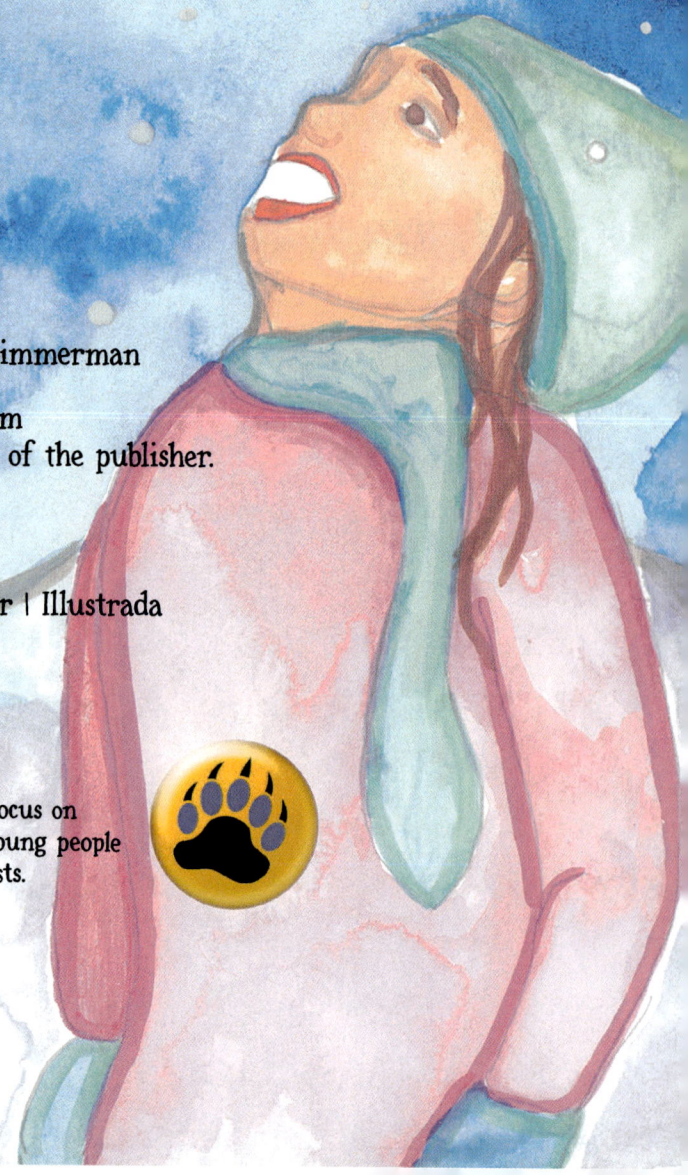

Made in the USA
Monee, IL
11 December 2023

47885348R00024